SO

SERIES
for very young readers

Books to read
yourself

For Lynne and Angela

Bertie Rooster

words: Maddie Stewart

pictures: Patrice Aggs

THE O'BRIEN PRESS
DUBLIN

First published 2003 by The O'Brien Press Ltd,
20 Victoria Road, Dublin 6, Ireland
Tel: +353 1 4923333; Fax: +353 1 4922777
E-mail: books@obrien.ie
Website: www.obrien.ie

ISBN: 0-86278-798-X

1 2 3 4 5 6 7 8 9 10
03 04 05 06 07 08 09 10

British Library Cataloguing-in-Publication Data
Stewart, Maddie
Bertie Rooster. - (Solo ; 2)
1.Sadness - Juvenile fiction 2.Helping behavior - Juvenile fiction
3.Chickens - Juvenile fiction 4.Children's stories
I.Title II.Aggs, Patrice
823.9'14[J]

Typesetting, layout, editing: The O'Brien Press Ltd
Printing: Stamford Press Pte Ltd (Singapore)

Bertie was a fine rooster.

Every morning at dawn
he crowed loudly.

'Cock-a-doodle-doo.
Cock-a-doodle-doo.'

He kept his
feathers **clean**.

He kept the hens
in order.

But that was **before** ...

... before the night
the **fox** got in
and nearly had Bertie
for his **supper**!

Farmer Mac had chased
the fox away
just in time.

After that,
Bertie was scared.

He hid in the corner
under the hay.

He didn't crow.

He didn't keep
his feathers clean.

He didn't even eat.

'That rooster is
no use,'
said the big white hen.

'No use at all,'

said the big red hen.

'No use at all,'

said the big black hen.

One morning, the farmer found a box at his door. Inside the box was a speckled hen.

There was a note with it.

Dear Farmer Mac,
This little hen has lost
her mother.
She is all alone.
Please look after her.
Sean

Farmer Mac took
the little hen
to the farmyard.

'What a **scrawny**
little thing!'
said the big hens.

The little speckled hen
cried very big tears.

'I wish I had
a **mummy**,'
she said.

Bertie heard
the little speckled hen.

'Don't worry, little hen,'
he said.
'I will look after you.'

'Will you be
my mummy?'
she said.

'I can't be your mummy,'
said Bertie.
'But I will be
your friend.'

Farmer Mac came
and scattered some corn.

The three big hens came
to gobble it all up.

But Bertie chased
them back.
'Give the little hen
a chance!' he said.

'Come with me,'
he said to the little hen.
'I'll show you around.'

He showed her
the old wrecked car.

He showed her
the duck pond.

'Quack, quack, quack,'
went the ducks.

He showed her the pig.
'Oink, oink, oink,'
went the pig.

He showed her
the hay store
and lots of places to hide.

All day,
the little speckled hen
followed Bertie
around the farmyard.

That night,
Farmer Mac came
to put the hens to bed.
'Bedtime!' he called.

'Quick, now, before
the **fox** comes
looking for his
supper.'

Farmer Mac counted
his birds.

There was
Bertie,
of course.

There was **Whitey**,
the big
white hen.

There was **Rose**,
the big
red hen.

There was **Blackie**,
the big
black hen.

**But where was
the little speckled hen?**

'Oh no!'
said Farmer Mac.
'I must find her
or the **fox** will have her
for his supper.'

He looked under
the old wrecked car.

But she
wasn't there.

He looked in
the hay store.
But she wasn't there.

He looked in the pig sty.
But she wasn't there.

He looked
down the lane
and he saw –

THE FOX.

'Scram! Scat!
Go catch a rat!'
said Farmer Mac.

And he chased
the fox away.

'He will be back soon,'
said Farmer Mac.

'I must close
the henhouse door.'

But what about
the little speckled hen?

'Goodnight, Whitey!'
said Farmer Mac.
'Buurk, buurk,' said
the big white hen.

'Goodnight, Rose!'
said Farmer Mac.
'Buurk, buurk,'
said the big
red hen.

'Goodnight, Blackie!'
said Farmer Mac.
'Buurk, buurk,'
said the big black hen.

'Goodnight, Bertie,'
said Farmer Mac.

'**Buurk, buurk,**'
said Bertie.

And then
Bertie lifted up
his wing.

'Buurk, buurk,'
said a little voice.

It was the
little speckled hen.

There she was,
safe and sound.

'Goodnight,
my little speckled hen,'
said Farmer Mac.

And they
all went to sleep.

Next morning,
Farmer Mac was
woken up at dawn.

'Cock-a-doodle-doo.
Cock-a-doodle-doo.'

'My Bertie is better,'
said Farmer Mac.

He smiled and
went back to sleep.